THE TALE OF THE BLACK UNICORN

by
Sandra Elaine Scott

Illustrations
by Jasmine Mills

The Tale of the Black Unicorn

Published by Vision Your Dreams
© 2020 Sandra Elaine Scott. All Rights Reserved

PRINTED IN THE UNITED STATES OF AMERICA
This book is a work of fiction. Names, characters, places, and incidents either are products of the author's imagination or are used fictitiously. Any resemblance to actual persons, living or dead, events, or locales is entirely coincidental.

Library of Congress Control Number: 2020911369
ISBN: 978-0-9969049-4-0

Author's Photograph ~ Audrey Andersen
Book Design ~ Karen White
Editors ~ Sandra James, Susan Rooks
Illustrator Photograph ~ Anthony Chatman

Visit the website: www.sandraelainescott.com

This book is dedicated
to children everywhere
who are different and
long to be accepted
just the way they are.

Reina was sad. The kids at school teased her. They made fun of her because she couldn't see very well and wore glasses. When the kids were really mean, they laughed at the dark color of her skin.

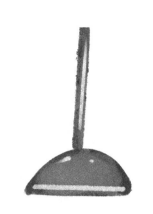

Reina moped all through dinner.

That night, as Reina snuggled in bed, her parents knew they needed to cheer her up. "Reina," Mama said, "we know you're feeling sad. We have just the story to make you feel better. Her dad whispered, "You are so special. We love you. It's time you heard the tale of the Black Unicorn."

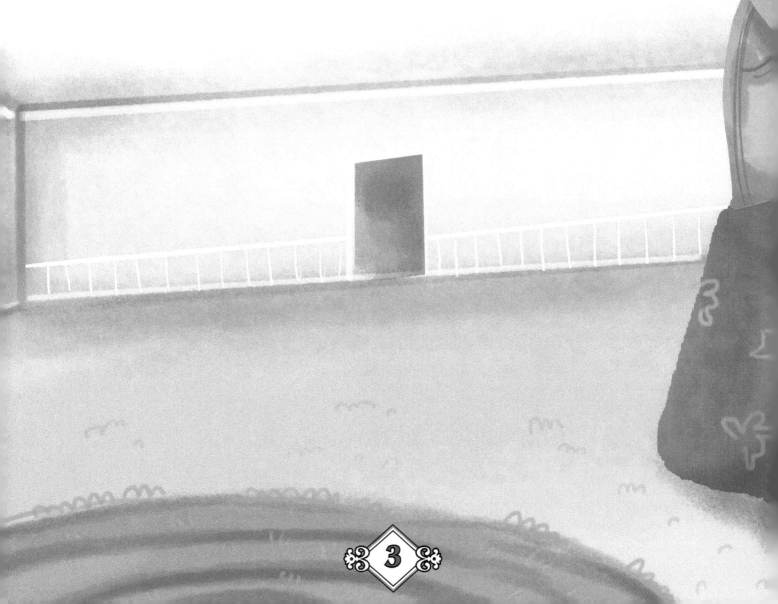

A long time ago in a distant land, there was a forest of magical unicorns. Each unicorn possessed powers such as love, kindness, imagination, bravery, joy, honesty, and wisdom. The unicorns always celebrated when a new unicorn was born. When this baby unicorn was born, they knew she too would have magical power, but they didn't know what it would be.

Her parents knew their baby was special; they were told in a dream that when she grew up she would be the Queen of unicorns. But they kept this a secret. They loved their baby unicorn and named her Reina. Each day, Reina's parents told her she was special.

As Reina grew up, she loved playing with all the other unicorns. They would play together and talk about what magical powers they had. But Reina didn't know what magical power she possessed, and that made her sad.

Then one day, strange things started to happen. Reina was walking by a meadow and saw some beautiful blades of grass. She started to play in the grass. She looked down and saw her hoofs were turning green. The other unicorns looked and pointed. "Oh my gosh, you're turning green!" they yelled.

Embarrassed, Reina ran home. Her parents were amazed and said "Wow, Reina, you are special among the unicorns! You are loved. You are beautiful. You are you."

A few days later, Reina saw a beautiful hummingbird hovering over the roses in the garden. She ran to meet the hummingbird and stopped to smell the roses. Then it happened again! Her nose turned red! Again, her friends yelled, "Now your nose is turning red!"

Reina ran home to her parents. Once again, they said "Wow, Reina, you are special among the unicorns! You are loved. You are beautiful. You are you."

Reina felt different than the other
unicorns. She walked alone into a
nearby orange grove, avoiding her
friends. She took a bite of orange and
noticed orange splotches showing up on
her coat. "Oh no!" she cried. "Not again!"

Reina rushed home. Her parents took one look at her and said, "Wow, Reina, you are special among the unicorns! You are loved. You are beautiful. You are you."

Reina looked in the mirror and saw red, green, and orange on her body. It started to rain, and Reina thought if she stood in the rain, the colors would wash off. But when Reina walked out into the rain, the dirt turned to mud. As Reina splashed in the mud, the mud got all over her, turning parts of her brown.

Reina ran back inside. She wanted to hide from her parents because she felt dirty, and parts of her were now brown. But when her parents saw her, they said, "Don't hide, Reina. You are special among the unicorns! You are loved. You are beautiful. You are you."

Before she went
to sleep that
night, Reina
stared up at
the night sky.
The sky was a
beautiful purple,
and Reina
admired how pretty
the sky was. Reina fell
asleep with a smile on her face because
she had asked the night sky to make her
just like the other unicorns.

But when she woke up, her coat
was now lined with purple stripes.

Once again, she rushed to her parents.
When her parents saw her, they said,
"Wow, Reina, you are special among
the unicorns! You are loved. You are
beautiful. You are you."

The next day, Reina
went on a visit to the sea.
She looked out at the beautiful blue water and
hoped that by jumping into the water all the
colors would wash off. Reina loved being in the
water and played and danced in the waves. At
first, the blue of the water showed up on her
body and then...

The waves crashed around her and off came the blue of the sea, the red of the flowers, the orange of the fruit, the green of the grass, the brown of the mud, and the purple of the night sky. The blended colors became one.

When Reina came out of the water, her
coat was beautiful and shiny. She was totally
Black. Reina ran all the way home, hiding
from all the other unicorns. She was afraid.
She no longer looked like the others.

Reina ran to her parents. With big smiles, they said, "Wow, Reina, you are special among the unicorns! You are loved. You are beautiful. You are you."

Reina knew her parents were trying to make her feel better. She stood outside to make a wish on a star to be just like all the other unicorns. The stars heard her and twinkled in delight. Suddenly, two stars fell from the sky and dropped their sparkle into her eyes. The stars whispered that she was beautiful.

The next morning, Reina stood between her parents as they welcomed the day. The sun called out to Reina, and she ran toward the horizon to greet it.

The sun sang to Reina, "You are loved.
You are beautiful. You are you! You are the
Black Unicorn. You are a gift to the world.
Stand tall and be proud of who you are.
Every creature on Earth will see themselves
in you and know they, too, are beautiful
and special just the way they are."

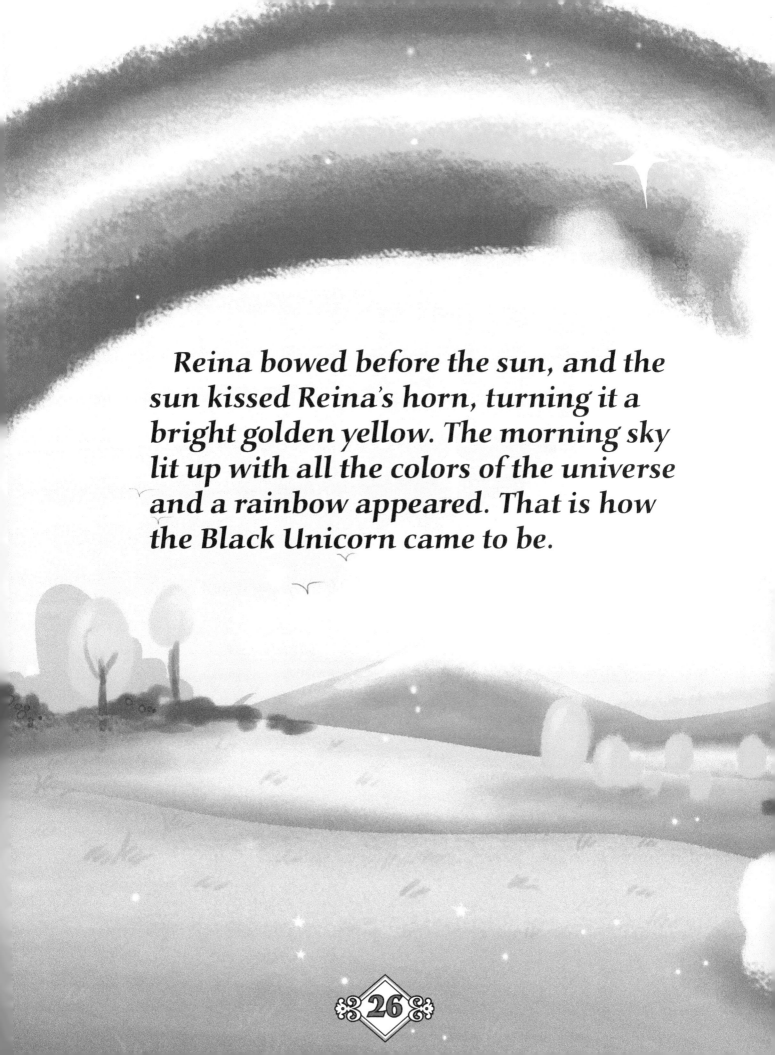

Reina bowed before the sun, and the sun kissed Reina's horn, turning it a bright golden yellow. The morning sky lit up with all the colors of the universe and a rainbow appeared. That is how the Black Unicorn came to be.

When Reina woke up the next morning, she now understood why she was named after the unicorn. She ran into her parents' bedroom, and said, "I remember listening to the bedtime story, but I fell asleep. I think I was dreaming because I saw Reina, the Black Unicorn. She was beautiful." Her parents smiled and said, "Reina, just like you!"

Reina walked into school feeling better about herself. She pictured Reina, the Black Unicorn, in her head, standing tall and proud. Reina smiled brightly and said "I am Loved. I am Beautiful. I am **ME!**"

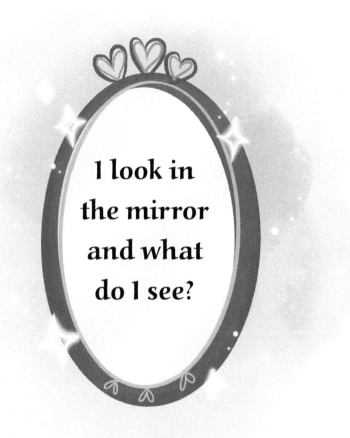

I look in
the mirror
and what
do I see?

Here are 3 awesome and positive things about me!

_____

_____

_____

The Magical Power of Thank You!

My magical power is to remember my manners and to say thank you to all the friends who helped me write this beautiful story.

A great big hug to these amazing individuals for their wisdom and insight: Alda, Angela, Bernadette, Darryl, Debbie, Gayle, Gloria, Judy, Kim, Maria, Mary'Beth, Natalie, Rolando, and Romi.

A high-five to my younger reading crew for their **very important** feedback: Emma, Hazel, Jack, and Natasha.

Thanks also to my amazing team of editors: Sandra James and Grammar Goddess Susan Rooks. And, of course, this book would be incomplete without the whimsical illustrations from Jasmine Mills and the book design of Karen White.

I also want to thank **YOU** for reading *The Tale of the Black Unicorn.* Always remember, "You are Loved, You are Beautiful, You are You!"

Muchísimas Gracias,

CPSIA information can be obtained
at www.ICGtesting.com
Printed in the USA
BVHW021740181220
595976BV00002B/81